A TRIP TO
MARS

DO NOT ENTER.
PREPARING
FOR TAKE OFF!

by Ruth Young
illustrated by Maryann Cocca-Leffler

Orchard Books   New York

Orchard Books
A division of Franklin Watts, Inc.
387 Park Avenue South
New York, NY 10016

Manufactured in the United States of America
Printed by General Offset Company, Inc.
Bound by Horowitz / Rae
Book design by Jean Krulis

The publisher gratefully acknowledges Francis Downey, Director of the Gengras Planetarium, Science
Museum of Connecticut, for his assistance in verifying the facts about Mars.

10 9 8 7 6 5 4 3 2 1

The text of this book is set in 21 pt. Cursivium Medium
The illustrations are acrylics, pastels, and colored pencil on d'Arches watercolor paper.

Library of Congress Cataloging-in-Publication Data
Young, Ruth, 1946-
A trip to Mars / by Ruth Young ; illustrated by Maryann Cocca-Leffler.
p.   cm.
Summary: A small child prepares for a trip to Mars, making sure to pack space gloves,
space glasses, and space teddy.
ISBN 0-531-05892-1. — ISBN 0-531-08492-2 (lib. bdg.)
[1. Space flight—Fiction.   2. Mars (Planet)—Fiction.]   I. Cocca-Leffler, Maryann,
1958-, ill.   II. Title.
PZ7.Y877Tr   1990   [E]—dc20   89-70936   CIP

There is only one way to make
a trip to Mars.

That is in a spaceship with silver wings an

many windows.

When you pack, don't forget your space suit!
You will need a space hat and space shoes.

Remember your space gloves, too.
Winters there are long and cold.

It doesn't rain on Mars, so you can
leave your space umbrella home.

But bring along a space mop....Mars
has dust storms!

Mars has two little moons—each one
much smaller than our moon.

But even with two, there's less light at night.
So bring along your flashlight.

Mars is called the red planet.
Its surface is dusty and covered with rust.
Winds blow the dust up into the Martian sky,
turning it pink.

Vegetables don't grow on Mars,
so you might bring some carrots.
And celery sticks are also great for a trip to Mars.

You can bring your space teddy
and a box of space cookies.
(Chocolate chip ones are the best.)
No one knows if there is life on Mars.
But just in case there is, bring some extra cookies.

Mars has clouds in its sky.
Some are white and wispy.
Others are reddish-orange,
probably from all that dust.
If you bring your space crayons,
you can make space pictures.

Mars is almost fifty million miles away.
Reading a space book on the way
will make the trip go faster.

Be sure to mark your space map
with an X where you live.
This will help you find your way home.

Before you leave, say goodbye to your parents.

BLAST OFF!

FACTS ABOUT MARS

Mars is the fourth planet in the solar system and the first planet beyond Earth. It is 141½ million miles from the sun—almost 50 million miles farther out than Earth. Since Mars is much farther from the sun, a Martian year is almost twice as long as an Earth year--about 687 Earth days. But a day on Mars is only 41 minutes longer than a day on Earth.

You can see Mars from Earth without a telescope, even though it is a small planet. Mars is the third smallest planet in our solar system, a little more than half as big as Earth.

EARTH MARS

Mars has two of the smallest moons in our solar system. They are named Phobos and Deimos. They are lumpy and odd-shaped, sort of like potatoes. They are smaller than our moon and reflect less light.

Since Mars has less mass than Earth, there is less gravity. If you weighed 100 pounds on Earth, you would weigh only 38 pounds on Mars.

Mars has a solid surface, but it's very rocky. There are craters, volcanoes, and mountains. One volcano is three times higher than Mount Everest. And the biggest valley is four times as deep as the Grand Canyon.

Mars is often called the red planet. It looks reddish-orange through a telescope and has white caps at its north and south poles. Most of the surface is covered with reddish-orange rust.

It doesn't rain on Mars. Sometimes gentle winds blow. Other times, winds stir up huge dust storms and the reddish-orange rust is swirled upward. These dust storms can engulf the entire planet.

Like Earth, Mars has four seasons, but its year is 23 Earth months long. It's much colder on Mars than on Earth most of the time. And even in the summer, it's sometimes freezing cold.

Mars has wispy clouds in its atmosphere. Some are whitish, like our clouds, others are reddish-orange, probably from those dust storms.

A human being couldn't breathe on Mars without a space helmet and an oxygen tank.

There is no free-flowing water on Mars. There are no rivers or streams. But there might have been, once. No vegetables grow on Mars, and no other form of life as we know it has been found.